Rain Forests
Surviving in the Amazon

by Michael Sandler
Consultant: Daniel H. Franck, Ph.D.

New York, New York

Credits

Cover, Robert Harding World Imagery/Getty Images; Title page, Robert Harding World Imagery/Getty Images; 4, Joel Sartore/National Geographic Image Collection; 5, Courtesy of Yossi Ghinsberg; 6, Steve Stankiewitz; 7, Martin Wendler/Photo Researchers, Inc.; 8, Steve Stankiewitz; 9(L), Noah Poritz/Photo Researchers, Inc.; 9(R), Scott Camazine/Photo Researchers, Inc.; 10(L), Ed George/National Geographic Image Collection; 10(R), Collart Herve/Corbis Sygma; 11, Gregory Ochocki/Photo Researchers, Inc.; 12, Victor Englebert/Photo Researchers, Inc.; 13, Herve Collart/Corbis Sygma; 14, Courtesy of Dr. Linnea Smith Amazon Medical Project; 15, Courtesy of Dr. Linnea Smith Amazon Medical Project; 16-17, Joel Sartore/National Geographic Image Collection; 18-19, Dave Herring; 20, George Grall/National Geographic Image Collection; 21, Jeanne White/Photo Researchers, Inc.; 22, Courtesy of Yossi Ghinsberg; 23, Courtesy of Yossi Ghinsberg; 24, Douglas Engle/Corbis; 25, Michael K. Nichols/National Geographic Image Collections; 26, Jacques Jangoux /Photo Researchers, Inc.; 27, © 2005 Sergio Ballivian; 29, Nature's Library/Photo Researchers, Inc.

EDITORIAL DEVELOPMENT by Judy Nayer
DESIGN AND PRODUCTION by Paula Jo Smith

Special thanks to Alan Perry at www.madidi.com

Library of Congress Cataloging-in-Publication Data

Sandler, Michael.
 Rain forests : surviving in the Amazon / by Michael Sandler.
     p. cm.—(X-treme places)
  Includes bibliographical references.
  ISBN 1-59716-089-X (library binding) — ISBN 1-59716-126-8 (pbk.)
 1. Rain forests—Amazon River Region—Juvenile literature. 2. Wilderness survival—Amazon River Region—Juvenile literature. I. Title. II. Series.
 QH112.S26 2006
 578.734′098—dc22
                    2005009977

Copyright © 2006 Bearport Publishing Company, Inc. All rights reserved. No part of this publication may be reproduced in whole or in part, stored in a retrieval system, or transmitted in any form or by any means, electronic, mechanical, photocopying, recording, or otherwise, without written permission from the publisher.

For more information, write to Bearport Publishing Company, Inc., 101 Fifth Avenue, Suite 6R, New York, New York 10003. Printed in the United States of America.

1 2 3 4 5 6 7 8 9 10

Contents

Lost!.. 4

What Is a Rain Forest? 6

Rain Forest Plants 8

Rain Forest Animals 10

People of the Rain Forest... 12

Helping Amazonians Survive................................... 14

Alone and Afraid 16

What Does It Take to Survive? 18

A Close Call 20

Saved!... 22

Rain Forests Under Attack...................................... 24

Saving the Rain Forest 26

Just the Facts.. 28

Glossary 30

Bibliography 31

Read More 31

Learn More Online 31

Index... 32

About the Author 32

Lost!

Yossi Ghinsberg woke with a start. He was in extreme pain. Insects were biting his legs. He reached down and grabbed one. In the darkness the insect felt like a giant ant. Yossi groaned. It was raining, and he had no way to protect himself. He was alone and lost in the Amazon rain forest.

Yossi had come to the rain forest with friends, ready for adventure. Now he had become separated from the group. Yossi had survived for over a week on his own. He didn't know how much longer he could go on, though.

During Yossi's journey, termites ate holes through some of his clothes.

In 1982, adventurer Yossi Ghinsberg was lost in the Amazon rain forest in Bolivia, a country in South America.

Rain Forest Plants

The variety of plant life in a rain forest is incredible. A patch of forest in the United States might have 10 or 12 different kinds of trees. The same size patch in a rain forest might have 200 species.

Layers of a Rain Forest

Emergent Layer— The layer made up of the tops of the tallest trees.

Canopy Layer— The layer containing most of the treetops.

Understory Layer— Little light comes through the canopy to reach this layer.

Forest Floor— Almost no plants grow on the dark forest floor.

The biggest problem for plants in the rain forest is getting enough sunlight. Almost no light **penetrates** the thick treetops. So plants are **adapted** to survive in this unique **environment**. Many plants grow on top of trees, rather than on the ground, to get light. Many plants also have wide leaves so they can take in more sunlight.

The rain forest is full of vines. These plants begin growing on the ground and then climb upward toward the sunlight.

Rosy periwinkle

Many rain forest plants contain ingredients that are used to make important medicines. For instance, the rosy periwinkle is used in a drug to treat childhood cancer.

9

Rain Forest Animals

The Amazon rain forest contains more species of animals than anywhere else in the world. All of them are adapted to living in or below the **dense** tangle of trees.

The rain forest is home to thousands of kinds of reptiles. The anaconda is the world's largest snake.

The six-inch (15-cm) tall pygmy marmoset is one of the world's smallest monkeys.

Many rain forest animal species are **endangered**. Many others have become extinct, or have died out completely. An average of 35 animal species become extinct in rain forests every day.

10

Various animal species live in the different layers of the rain forest. Many birds live in the emergent layer, where they can fly freely. Monkeys enjoy climbing and leaping in the canopy. Frogs and jaguars enjoy the cool, damp environment of the understory. Giant anteaters live on the forest floor.

Insects make up the largest group of rain forest animals. There are millions of different kinds of insects in the Amazon rain forest.

The Amazon River dolphin is one of over 400 kinds of mammals found in the Amazon rain forest.

People of the Rain Forest

People have lived in the Amazon rain forest for over 10,000 years. During that time, they have depended on the rain forest to provide for their needs.

The Yanomami (*ya*-noh-MA-mee) are the largest group of Amazonian Indians living in the rain forest. Before the 1980s, the Yanomami had very little contact with the outside world.

Today, many Yanomami live the same way they have for thousands of years.

Most Yanomami live in small villages deep within the forest. They survive by hunting, fishing, and gathering fruits and nuts. They also clear areas of land to plant crops.

Yanomami children

In the 1500s, millions of Yanomami lived in the Brazilian Amazon. Today, less than 200,000 live in the region. Diseases brought by European settlers caused much of the population loss.

Helping Amazonians Survive

Most Amazonian Indians are poor. They live without electricity, running water, or medical care. Dr. Linnea Smith is trying to help them.

Dr. Smith first visited the Amazon while on vacation. She fell in love with the rain forest and decided she had to return. When she did, she set up a medical **clinic** on the Amazon River. Today, Dr. Smith's clinic sees around 2,000 patients per year.

Dr. Smith at her clinic

The wildlife around Dr. Smith constantly reminds her that she is in the heart of the Amazon. One afternoon, a 20-foot (6-m) anaconda was pulled from the river outside the clinic.

Dr. Smith's patients live deep in the rain forest. Normally, they would not be able to see a doctor.

There are no roads leading to the medical clinic. Everything Dr. Smith needs, including her patients, must come by boat or plane.

Alone and Afraid

In the rain forest, people depend on one another for survival. Yossi didn't have anyone. He only had a few supplies, such as a lighter to make fires at night. He also had a **poncho** and a flashlight. However, he had no tent and almost no food. He ate fruit from trees or small fish from the river. He went days without eating.

Every step Yossi took was painful. The dampness of the rain forest had kept his feet from drying properly. Now they were **infected**.

Still, Yossi kept walking. He followed the river in hopes of finding a village.

The Tuichi (TWEE-chee) River is one of the many small rivers that run through the Bolivian rain forest before joining the mighty Amazon River. The Tuichi is a wild river with powerful **rapids**.

What Does It Take to Survive?

Surviving in the Amazon can be tough. Dense plant growth and heavy rains make travel difficult. Villages are few and far between, so it is hard to find help if you become lost.

For those who don't know where to look, finding food can be very difficult. Many rain forest insects and animals are poisonous. Eating the wrong one could be **fatal**.

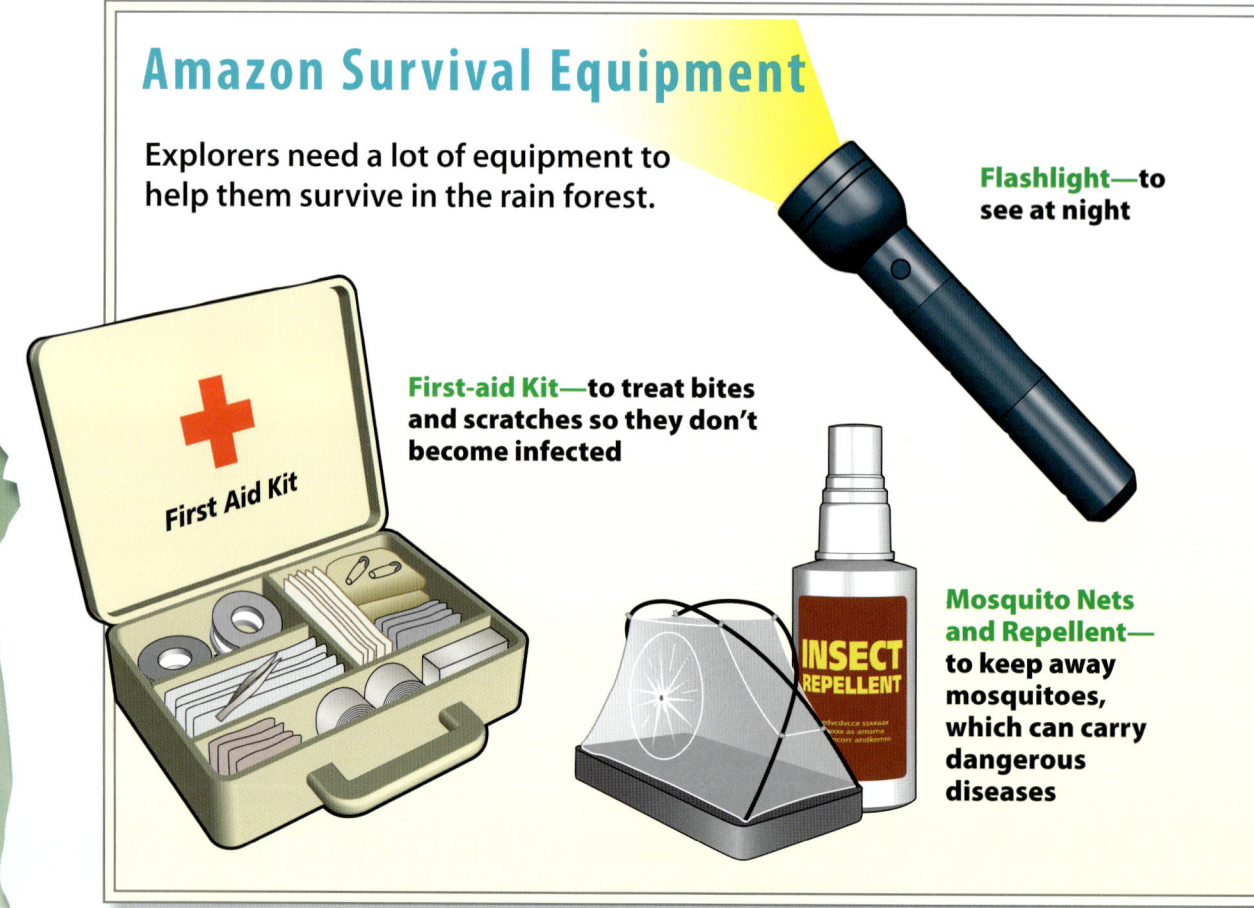

Amazon Survival Equipment

Explorers need a lot of equipment to help them survive in the rain forest.

Flashlight—to see at night

First-aid Kit—to treat bites and scratches so they don't become infected

Mosquito Nets and Repellent—to keep away mosquitoes, which can carry dangerous diseases

Some animals are harmful in other ways. At dawn and dusk, mosquitoes swarm and bite. Fire ants give painful stings. Jaguars or wild boars may attack. The bite from a poisonous snake can be deadly.

Machete—for cutting a path through the forest and for finding food

Water Filter—for making river water safe to drink

Long Pants and Long-sleeved Shirt—to keep arms and legs covered to help prevent bites and scratches

Many adventurers have lost their lives exploring the Amazon. Of the four people in Yossi's group, only two survived.

A Close Call

One night, Yossi heard leaves rustling near the ground where he lay. He sat up, switched on his flashlight, and came face-to-face with a jaguar.

Jaguars are the largest cats in the Americas. To many Amazonian Indians, the jaguar is the most feared and admired of all the rain forest animals.

Yossi managed to scare the jaguar away. He was shaken, though. Now he knew just how dangerous it was to be in the rain forest alone.

Even though he was starving, Yossi had to be careful to avoid meals like this poison dart frog.

Saved!

One evening, Yossi heard what sounded like a motor. He thought he was dreaming. By this time he had been alone in the jungle for three weeks.

Yossi, moments after he was rescued

The noise grew louder. It was coming from the river right behind him. Yossi went down to the riverbank. Three men in a motorized canoe were coming upriver toward him. One of the men was his friend Kevin. Yossi had been separated from Kevin on the river weeks ago, when their raft **capsized**. Now Kevin had come to rescue him. Yossi was saved!

Yossi couldn't believe he had survived. He knew his life would never be the same.

Today, Yossi travels the world as a public speaker, telling audiences about his experience.

Yossi's experience in the Amazon was a turning point in his life. He wrote a book about it called *Back from Tuichi*.

Rain Forests Under Attack

People are cutting down rain forests at alarming rates. Some want land for farming or raising cows. Others want the trees for their valuable wood. In the Amazon, **mining** is also a problem. Mining destroys land. Also, the chemicals used in mining can kill plants and animals.

Every second, the world is losing an area of rain forest about the size of two football fields. At this rate, all of the world's rain forests could be gone in less than 50 years.

When a single rain forest tree is cut down, 500 plants, animals, and insects can lose their home.

The Amazon is losing almost 8,000 square miles (12,875 sq km) of rain forest per year. The Congo Basin rain forest in Africa, the world's second largest, is shrinking by 3,000 square miles (4,828 sq km) per year.

A demand for valuable rain forest wood means that people keep cutting down trees.

Saving the Rain Forest

Yossi was thankful that he survived in the Amazon rain forest. He wanted the rain forest to survive as well. After being rescued, Yossi helped start the Chalalan Project. This group made the area where Yossi was lost a **nature reserve** for tourists.

One reason rain forests are important is that they make oxygen for humans to breathe.

All over the world, people and governments are working together to save rain forests. They realize that losing such an important part of the planet would cause huge problems.

People also want to **preserve** the incredible beauty of rain forests. The Amazon touches all those who experience it. As Yossi says, "The beauty of the place makes one's heart sing."

This kitchen was built as part of the Chalalan Project.

Some countries have created protected areas within their rain forests. These are places where people cannot cut down, burn, or damage the trees in any other way.

Just the Facts

MORE ABOUT THE AMAZON AND OTHER RAIN FORESTS

- The Amazon rain forest covers about two-thirds the size of the United States.

- How wet are the rain forests? Compare the amount of rain the Amazon gets with the area where you live. The graph below shows the amount of rain different places in the United States receive.

- The Amazon River, which cuts through the Amazon rain forest, is one of the biggest rivers in the world. It travels about 4,000 miles (6,437 km) from its source in northern Peru before draining into the Atlantic Ocean in Brazil. Though not as long as Africa's Nile River, the Amazon carries more water than any other river in the world.

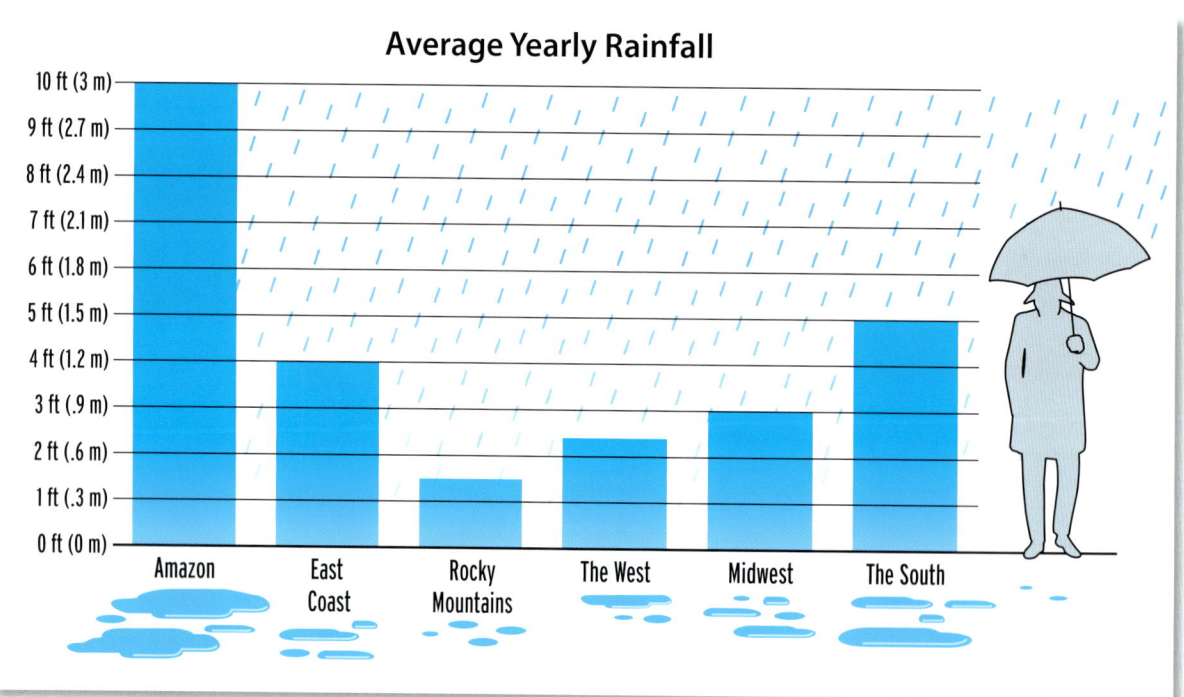

- Many foods originally grew wild in the rain forest. These include avocados, bananas, cocoa, black pepper, cinnamon, coffee, eggplants, lemons, peanuts, sugar, tomatoes, rice, and vanilla beans.

- Many North American birds spend their winters in the South and Central American rain forests. As these rain forests disappear, fewer birds can make it through the winter.

- There are over 1,000 different species of butterflies in the Amazon rain forest.

One of the Amazon's many types of butterflies

GLOSSARY

adapted (uh-DAP-tid) changed because of the environment or conditions; changed over time to be fit for the environment

capsized (KAP-sized) turned over in the water

clinic (KLIN-ik) a place where people can go for medical treatment

dense (DENSS) thick

endangered (en-DAYN-jurd) in danger of dying out

environment (en-VYE-ruhn-muhnt) the plants, animals, and weather in a place

equator (i-KWAY-tur) an imaginary line around the middle of Earth

fatal (FAY-tuhl) deadly

humid (HYOO-mid) moist and damp

infected (in-FEK-tid) injured and filled with germs

mining (MINE-ing) digging up minerals that are underground

nature reserve (NAY-chur ri-ZURV) a place where animals and plants are protected

penetrates (PEN-uh-trates) goes inside or through

poncho (PON-choh) a loose coat that is like a blanket with a hole in the center for a person's head

preserve (pri-ZURV) to protect

rapids (RA-pidz) a fast-moving part of a river

species (SPEE-sheez) types of animals or plants

BIBLIOGRAPHY

Bernard, Hans-Ulrich. *Insight Guide Amazon Wildlife.* Singapore: APA Publications (2002).

Capelas, Jr., Afonso. *Amazonia: The Land, the Wildlife, the River, the People.* Toronto: Firefly Books (2003).

The Cousteau Society. *An Adventure in the Amazon.* New York: Simon & Schuster (1992).

Ghinsberg, Yossi. *Back from Tuichi: The Harrowing Life-and-Death Story of Survival in the Amazon Rainforest.* New York: Random House (1993).

Parker, Janice, ed. *The Disappearing Forests.* North Mankato, MN: Smart Apple (2002).

Smithsonian Tropical Research Institute: striweb.si.edu/rainforest/

READ MORE

Gibbons, Gail. *Nature's Green Umbrella: Tropical Rain Forests.* New York: HarperTrophy (1997).

Goodman, Susan E. *Ultimate Field Trip #1: Adventures in the Amazon Rain Forest.* New York: Aladdin (1999).

Montgomery, Sy. *Encantado: Pink Dolphin of the Amazon.* Boston: Houghton Mifflin (2002).

Platt, Richard. *The Vanishing Rainforest.* London: Frances Lincoln (2004).

Telford, Carole, and Rod Theodorou. *Up a Rainforest Tree.* Chicago: Heinemann Library (2001).

LEARN MORE ONLINE

Visit these Web sites to learn more about the Amazon and rain forests:

www.greatestplaces.org/book_pages/amazon2.htm

www.pbs.org/journeyintoamazonia/

www.rainforest-alliance.org/programs/education/kids/resources.html

www.zoomschool.com/subjects/rainforest/

INDEX

Africa 25, 28
Amazon River 14, 17, 28
Amazonian Indians 12–13, 14, 20
anaconda 10, 15
animals 7, 10–11, 18–19, 20, 24
anteaters 11
ants 4, 19

Back from Tuichi 23
birds 11, 29
Bolivia 5, 6–7, 17
Brazil 6–7, 13, 28
butterflies 29

canopy 8, 11
Central America 6, 29
Chalalan Project 26–27
Congo Basin 25
Costa Rica 6

dolphins 11

endangered animals 10
equator 6
European settlers 13
extinct animals 10

food 16, 18–19, 29
frogs 11, 21

Ghinsberg, Yossi 4–5, 16–17, 19, 20–21, 22–23, 26–27

insects 4, 11, 18, 24

jaguars 11, 19, 20–21

Madagascar 6
medical clinic 14–15
medicines 9
mining 24
monkeys 10–11
mosquitoes 18–19

nature reserve 26
Nile River 28
North America 29

Peru 7, 28
plants 7, 8–9, 18, 24
pygmy marmoset 10

rain 4, 7, 18, 28

Smith, Dr. Linnea 14–15
snakes 10, 19
South America 5, 6, 29
species 7, 8, 10–11, 29
survival equipment 18–19

temperature 7
trees 6, 8–9, 10, 16, 24–25, 27
tropics 6
Tuichi River 17

United States 8, 28

West Africa 6
wild boars 19

Yanomami 12–13

ABOUT THE AUTHOR

Michael Sandler lives in Brooklyn, New York, with his family. He has written many books for children and young adults. An avid traveler, he says that one of his favorite trips was a safari through the Bolivian Amazon.